The Boy
on the Porch

SHARON CREECH

The Boy on the Porch

JOANNA COTLER BOOKS
An Imprint of HarperCollins *Publishers*

Library of Congress Cataloging-in-Publication Data is available.
ISBN 978-0-06-189235-6 (trade bdg.) — ISBN 978-0-06-189237-0 (lib. bdg.)

Typography by Kate Engbring
13 14 15 16 17   XXXXXX   10 9 8 7 6 5 4 3 2 1

First Edition

Dedication to come

I

The young couple found the child asleep in an old cushioned chair on the front porch. He was curled against a worn pillow, his feet bare and dusty, his clothes fashioned from rough linen. They could not imagine where he had come from or how he had made his way to their small farmhouse on a dirt road far from town.

"How old a boy is he, do you think?" the man asked.

"Hard to say, isn't it? Seven or eight?"

"Small for his age then."

"Six?"

"Big feet."

"Haven't been around kids much."

"Me neither."

The man circled the house and then walked down the dirt drive, past their battered blue truck and the shed, scanning the bushes on both sides as he went. Their dog, a silent beagle, slipped into his place beside the man, sniffing the ground earnestly.

When the man and the dog returned to the porch, the woman was kneeling beside the old cushioned chair, her hand resting gently on the boy's back. There was something in the tilt of her head and the tenderness of her touch that moved him.

The young couple, Marta and John, were reluctant to go about their normal chores, fearing that the boy would wake and be afraid, and so they took turns watching over the sleeping boy. It did not seem right to wake him.

For several hours, they moved about more quietly than usual, until at last John said, "It is time to wake that child, Marta. Maybe he is sick, sleeping so much like that."

"You think so?" She felt his forehead, but it was cool, not feverish.

They made small noises: they coughed and tapped their feet upon the floor, and they let the screen door flap shut in its clumsy way, but still the child slept.

"Tap him," John said. "Tap him on the back."

She tapped him lightly at first, and then more firmly, as if she were patting a drum. Nothing.

"Lift him up," John said.

"Oh, no, I couldn't. You do it."

"No, no, it might scare him to see a big man like me. You do it. You're more gentle."

Marta blushed at this and considered the child and what might be the best way to lift him.

"Just scoop him up," John said.

She scooped up the boy in one swift move, but he was heavier than she had expected, and she swayed and turned and flopped into the chair with the boy now in her arms.

Still the boy slept.

Marta looked up at John and then down at the dusty-headed boy. "I suppose I'd better just sit here with him until he wakes," she said.

The sight of his wife with the child in her lap made John feel peculiar. He felt joy and surprise and worry and fear all at once, in such a rush, making him dizzy.

"I'll tend to the cows," he said abruptly. "Call me if you need me."

Her chin rested on the child's head; her hand pat-patted his back.

"It's okay," Marta whispered to the sleeping child. "I will sit here all day, if need be."

Their dog normally shadowed John from dawn until dusk, but on this day, he chose to lie at Marta's feet, eyes closed, waiting. Before John went to the barn, he scanned the drive again and circled their farmhouse. Finding nothing out of the ordinary, he hurried on to his chores.

Marta closed her eyes. "It's okay, it's okay," she whispered.

3

She must have dozed off, for she was startled by something tapping her face.

The child's hand rested on her cheek, his eyes wide, a deep, dark brown, and his face so close to hers that she had to lean back to focus.

"Oh!" Marta said. "Don't be afraid. We found you here, on the porch, don't be afraid."

He gazed back at her steadily and then turned to take in the porch, the trees beyond, and the beagle at his feet. He let his hand drop toward the beagle—not reaching for the dog, but as if offering his hand in case the dog should want to sniff it.

The beagle sniffed the hand and then the boy's

arms and legs. He licked the dust from the boy's feet.

"I am Marta," she said. "What are you called?"

The boy made no motion to move from her lap and he did not answer.

"You must be hungry," Marta said. "Would you like something to eat? To drink?"

The boy looked out at the bushes, the drive.

4

The boy followed Marta into the house and stood beside her as she cut a thick slice of bread, drizzled it with honey, and set it on a plate beside a ripe pear and a glass of milk. His appetite seemed good, for he ate what was on the plate and licked the honey off his finger. Again he offered his hand to the beagle, letting the dog lick the honey.

"Now," Marta said, "can you tell me your name?"

The boy's fingers tapped on the table.

"Can you tell me how you came here? Did someone bring you?"

The boy looked at her pleasantly enough and tapped his fingers lightly on the table, but he said nothing.

When John returned from the barn, the boy regarded him casually. The boy looked all around the room, equally interested, it seemed, in the man and woman standing before him as in the table, the dog, the wooden cabinet, the washbasin, the cupboards.

"Look, John, the boy woke up." Her words sounded silly to her ears.

"Yes, yes, I see," John said, smiling. His voice had boomed out of his mouth, much too loud. "And what might your name be, boy?" Still too loud.

The boy licked his lips, tapped his fingers on the table.

"He won't say, John. I've tried already."

"Is he deaf, do you think?"

"No, he seems to hear all right. He just doesn't speak."

"Probably too shy," John said. "That's okay, boy, take your time getting used to us." He turned to his wife. "No one's come for him yet?"

"No, shh, no."

"Surely someone will come for him, Marta."

"Shh."

The boy reached into his pocket, withdrew a crumpled note, and handed it to Marta.

* * *

Plees taik kair of Jacob.

9

He is a ~~god~~ good boy.
Wil be bak wen we can.

5

When no one had come for the boy by nightfall, John and Marta fashioned a small bed beside their own. Marta offered the boy one of John's softest shirts to sleep in and set out a basin of warm water and soap for him to wash with. She tucked him into the bed, patted his hand, and hummed a few bars of an old, half-forgotten lullaby, softly, for she was embarrassed that John might hear her and think her foolish. As she stood to go, the boy reached up and tapped her arm five or six times, in that funny way he did, always lightly tapping on surfaces, on his own arm, on the dog, on the floor. His touch startled her, and she nearly wept, so grateful was she for the gesture.

After the child was asleep, John said, "This is too strange, Marta. Are you sure you have no idea who—"

"No! No idea. Maybe someone you worked for? Maybe a distant relative?"

"No, no. Maybe one of *your* relatives?"

"You know they have no idea where we live. My family never kept track of anybody."

"But then, who?"

"And why *us*?"

"I thought they'd be back by evening, didn't you?"

"Yes."

"Surely by tomorrow then."

"Surely."

6

At noon the next day, John said, "Marta, I don't know about all this. What are we supposed to do with the boy?"

Marta stood on the back porch, watching the child trail a stick through the dirt. The beagle followed close behind, sniffing at the ground.

"Marta? Should I take the boy with me when I go to town?"

"No. The people might come back."

"What people?"

"The people who left the note. The ones who said they'd be back."

"But they didn't say *when* they'd be back, did they?

They didn't say that."

After John left for town, Marta took the boy to the barn to see the new kittens and the mother goat and her three-month-old babes. The boy petted the animals and mimicked the kittens skittering and the goats leaping. The beagle watched from the side, intervening only when the boy got too close to the mother goat. When the boy sat in the straw, the kittens crawled over him and the young goats butted their heads under his arms, making the child laugh.

But it was a silent laugh, a laugh that you could see but not hear. It spread across his face and shook his body; it waggled his arms and legs. It was Marta who gave voice to the laugh, watching the boy. She laughed until her side ached; she laughed until the beagle crawled up into her lap and licked her face, as if to taste the laugh. And as she was laughing, Marta was hoping that the boy might stay a day or two.

During the twelve-mile stretch into town, John's mind took as many winding turns as the narrow road. He tried to ready himself for what he might hear in town and for what he should say. Maybe he should go straight to the sheriff's office and let him know about the boy. He didn't like the sheriff much. He was a bossy man, given to poking his finger in your face as if to warn you that he knew better about everything and you'd better not waste his time.

John's mind turned to Marta's face when she held the child and when she'd tucked him into bed and when she'd risen in the night to check on him. Maybe, John thought, he should first go to the general store and pick up the tone of things. Gossip found its way quickly to the general store in these small towns.

Out of nowhere, he thought of jelly beans and how he'd loved them as a child, how his father had taken him into town and let him buy a nickel's worth of jelly beans from the glass jar on the counter at the general store.

Maybe, John thought, he would bring home some jelly beans for the boy.

7

When John returned home, the farmhouse was empty. He dashed out into the yard and called for Marta. He raced to the barn, calling her name. "Marta! Marta!"

He didn't know what made him so anxious. Maybe the people had come for the boy. He should have stayed home with Marta. What if there was a problem—but what sort of problem? What was the matter with him? He wasn't usually a worrier.

The barn was empty, except for kittens bouncing over hay bales. The goats and cows were in the fenced enclosures outdoors. And then he saw them, Marta and the boy, at the far end of the enclosure, lining up bottles and cans on the fence.

"John, there you are—what news? Oh, don't tell me. Please don't tell me. Listen to this—"

The boy raised his hands as if he were a music conductor, and then he began tapping at the bottles and cans with slender sticks. It wasn't random, reckless tapping: there was a distinct rhythm to it, slow and soft at first, rising to a crescendo, and then falling back to beautiful calm and then rising again. It sounded like waves at the ocean or the wind as it came across the fields and through the trees.

"I taught him that!" Marta said. "I mean, I was pretending to be a conductor and he put the cans up there and then—oh, I don't know—I was just tapping them—"

"You were pretending to be a conductor? You were tapping the cans?"

"Well, don't sound so *surprised*, John."

"But how would you know how to be a—oh, never mind."

"The boy was imitating my every move and then he took off with it. Listen to him."

The boy continued, oblivious to everything but the sounds coming from the bottles and cans.

"And wait," Marta said. "Watch what he does with the ladder."

Farther down the fence was a ladder which she now dragged toward the boy. She handed the boy thicker sticks—ones John had used for stirring paint.

"I taught him this!" she said.

The boy rapped a rhythmic tune against the wooden ladder, on the sides and the rungs, a livelier, louder rhythm, full of life and joy, like a dozen dancers dancing on a wooden floor, or a dozen drummers drumming.

"You taught him that?" John asked.

"Only part—just the beginning—and he makes up the rest. He's very quick to learn, John."

Next the boy's attention moved on to a bucket half full of rainwater. He dipped a stick into the bucket and swirled the water round and round.

"If it's bad news from town, don't tell me, John. Not yet."

He rested a hand on her shoulder. "There is bad news and there is good news."

"Don't tell me the bad news, John."

"The bad news is—"

Marta covered her ears. "I said don't tell me—"

John moved her hands. "—that you've got cat poo on your skirt—and the good news is that there's no news in town."

"No news? No news at all?"

"Well, now, I take that back. There was a little news. Vernie Gossem broke his leg, kicking his cow."

"Serves him right then. Kicking his cow!"

"I brought something for the boy," John said, removing a small brown bag from his jacket pocket and opening it for Marta to see its contents. He glanced away, embarrassed.

"John, don't you go filling this boy up with too many sweets."

"You're one to talk. Didn't I see a batch of newly made fudge on the counter?"

"I don't know what you're talking about. Go ahead now, see if he likes those jelly beans."

The boy—Jacob—seemed reluctant to take the jelly beans that John offered him, but at last he held a few in his hand and stared at them.

"Doesn't he know what they are?" Marta said.

John reached into the bag, selected a red jelly bean, and popped it into his own mouth. "Mm," he said. "Mmm, mm."

The boy chose a red jelly bean from his palm and placed it on his tongue. He tapped his lips twice and smiled.

8

That night, after the boy had fallen asleep, Marta said, "I just can't imagine how anyone could drop off their child at a complete stranger's house—can you, John? What on earth could they have been thinking?"

"Maybe they had an emergency."

"But why leave him *here*? It doesn't make a bit of sense."

"He still hasn't spoken?"

"Not a word out of him. Do you think he's simply not *able* to speak?"

"Marta, I don't know the answer to that. I don't know what to make of this boy."

They'd both been puzzled by the boy's silence and equally puzzled by the boy's inclination to rap and tap on nearly every surface with sticks and spoons and whatever object was nearest. He tapped cups on saucers and a comb on a basin; he tapped book against book and stone against stone; and if there was no object at hand, there were always his hands and his feet patting and flicking and rapping and drumming.

"Maybe it is just what boys do," Marta said. "Did you do that when you were young, John?"

"I don't think so, no. Maybe sometimes, maybe if I had a stick in my hand . . ." It was hard to remember himself as a boy. Sometimes it hardly seemed possible that he'd ever been a boy at all, but . . . at other times, he felt he was *still* a boy and he was surprised to be in this man's body, married and all, with a wife and responsibilities. How had that happened exactly?

"John, we should stop calling him 'boy.' It isn't right. It makes him sound—I don't know—unimportant."

At that, the beagle nudged John's leg, as if to say, *What about me? What about me?*

"We don't have a name for our dog, do we, Marta? And he's not unimportant."

"He does so have a name: Beagle."

"But he *is* a beagle, Marta."

"I know, and that's why it's a good name for him."

Then "Boy" should be a good enough thing to call a boy, John thought, but he didn't say so because as soon as he thought it, he knew it wasn't true. "Boy" was not a good enough thing to call a boy.

"His name is Jacob, and that's what we should call him."

"When do you think the people will come back for him?"

"Soon, don't you think? Surely, soon."

9

John could not sleep. First, he was thinking that he should go to the sheriff's office and report the boy's arrival. But the sheriff would just make a mess of things, scaring the boy, scaring Marta. Maybe the people would come tomorrow. Maybe he should stop worrying. He was not a worrier. Why was he worrying so much?

Then he thought about names. *Your name is important.* Your name makes a statement about you. It describes not only who you are but who you might be.

Could he—John—have been named Franklin or Carter or Richmond or Conrad? No, too formal. Dwight or Thaddeus? No, no.

Matthew, Mark, or Luke? No. Billy? Willy? Charlie? Sammy? No, he wasn't one of those, either. He was John: solid, reliable, kind John.

He wondered what *Jacob* was. The name was not unlike John's. He was glad of that, although he couldn't have said why.

Marta was also awake. She was remembering earlier in the day when Jacob had found a piece of stiff wire fencing and was using it to tap against the stones and bottles and cans, and the sounds that emerged were so beautiful and clear and pure that it seemed as if the boy had been destined to be in this place at this time. Maybe the people would stay away a few more days.

IO

The road at the end of their drive was not heavily traveled and only rarely did a vehicle turn onto their property, usually with a driver who was lost and seeking directions. John and Marta used to welcome these interruptions into the sameness of their days, but now they were wary of intrusions, alert to the sound of cars or trucks on the road, wondering if this next one would bring back "the people."

But on the fourth day of the child's stay, John said, "This is not right, Marta. We must let someone know the boy is here."

Marta knew this. She knew the boy would have to leave. But so soon?

"Marta, you don't think he was kidnapped, do you?"

"Kidnapped? But then why would he be dropped off here?"

"Well, then, maybe the people who dropped him off got lost coming back to get him. Maybe they couldn't find us again."

And so that day, as Marta and the boy made their way to the barn to feed the animals, John set off down the winding road to town once more.

This time, in the general store, as John was paying for his purchases, he asked the owner, Shep Martin, if there'd been any talk of a lost boy.

"What kind of lost boy would you be talking about?" Shep asked. Shep was a thin, bald-headed man with a potbelly that hung over his belt like a sack of feed. He didn't like using two words where ten or twelve might do. "Would you be talking about a teenage kind of boy wandering around drunk and can't find his stupid way home? Or would you be talking about a younger sort of squirt who ran away? Or—"

"Younger."

"Can't say as I've heard anybody talking about that, no, I can't, except for maybe Vernie's grandson, you know the one I mean? The redheaded one with the tattoos?

Lord knows why a person would mess up his skin like that—"

"Is Vernie's grandson lost?"

"Lost in the head, that's what Vernie says. Is that the kind of lost boy you mean?"

"No."

"Would you be looking for a lost boy? What do you need with a lost boy?"

John scooped up his purchases and waved away the questions. "Naw, Shep, I thought I heard somebody mention it. I must've misunderstood. Maybe they were talking about—ha-ha—lost *parents*. You hear anything about any lost parents?"

"Lost *parents*? Would you be looking for lost parents? Why ever—"

"Naw, Shep, naw. Bye, now."

From there, John drove to the sheriff's office but sat in his truck for ten minutes before mustering the will to enter. Inside, he scanned the Most Wanted posters and the handwritten notices tacked to the bulletin board.

> *LOST: My cow's gone off again,*
> *you know the one. Vernie.*

No dumping in the church dumpster! We mean it!

FOUND: two black kittens by the creek, I'll keep
them if you don't want them back and I know
you don't or you wouldn't have dumped them
there in the 1st place. Darlene.

Darlene, who also happened to be the sheriff's receptionist, asked John what he was looking for.

"Thought I heard tell of a lost boy," John said.

"You lose a boy or find a boy?"

John had not expected such a direct question. "I saw a boy—"

"Well, honey, haven't we all? Haven't we all?"

John turned to leave. "Saw a boy the other day, looked lost, but if nobody's looking for a lost boy, I must've been mistaken."

"Lots of boys look lost."

John was relieved to leave town. He'd made an honest effort, not the biggest effort, it was true, but he'd tried.

11

"Don't tell me if it's bad news," Marta said. "Is it? Is it bad?"

"It's bad if you're Vernie Gossem. Now he's lost his cow."

"But—"

"But it's good if you're hoping no one has reported a lost boy."

"No one has reported him missing?"

"That's right, and I also asked about lost parents, but there don't seem to be any of those, either. Where's the boy—Jacob—now?"

"Up with the goats. I've just come down to get us a snack. John, we have something to show you—you are not going to believe your eyes!"

Up in the barn, the boy was at one end, wielding a two-inch paintbrush. At his feet were two half-used cans of paint. On the wall he had painted a tall blue tree with a white swing. All around the tree were swirls of blue, like bubbles floating in the air.

"I didn't do any of it," Marta said proudly. "He did it all."

"A blue tree?"

12

John and Marta owned two cows—received in payment for helping Vernie Gossem build an addition to his house—and a calf that was born about the same time as the baby goats. The elder cows were docile creatures, swinging their big heads slowly as they ate. The calf was still wobbly-legged, like the baby goats, and often the calf and goats would wobble and gambol around the pasture, bashing into each other clumsily.

Like their beagle, the cows and goats, cats and kittens did not have names. Marta had thought this a little odd, but John had told her it felt silly to give them names. "You'd run out of names if you named every animal," he had said.

On the morning after John had been to town again, he and Marta heard the low mooing of a cow, but they knew instantly it was not their own, and besides, the sound was not coming from the barn or the pasture. It was drifting up from the road.

"It's probably Vernie's wandering cow," John said, putting on his boots.

"If it is, you get that cow away from here, John. We don't want nosy Vernie poking around."

From the curve halfway down the drive, John could see the fence and the road just beyond.

"What the—?" The cow was near the road, as he'd suspected, but it wasn't roaming loose. It was tied firmly to his fence. John looked up and down the road. He examined the cow: a sturdy one, well-fed, with a sleek coat and bright eyes. He'd seen Vernie's cow and this wasn't it.

Two hours later, the cow was still there, and she was still there after lunch when John returned to retrieve her and lead her up to the barn.

To Marta, he said, "Looks like we've got more company."

13

Two years earlier, when John and Marta had found the beagle lying in the shade on their porch, they hadn't thought much about how it came to be there. It had no collar, its ribs shone through its dusty coat, and they assumed the dog to be another stray from an unwanted litter. They didn't expect the dog to stick around, but it did, day after day, week after week, until it seemed as if the dog had always been there, so easily did he fit in, following John from chore to chore, leaning against Marta's ankles as she prepared meals, curling up at the foot of their bed protectively, and looking at them endearingly with those big, black eyes.

When John and Marta had found the boy on

the porch, they were curious, naturally, as to why he was there—and they hadn't expected him to stay, not at first, but he did stay, day after day, until it seemed as if he belonged, running and smiling and laughing his silent laugh, tapping and patting on every surface as he made his music, and painting—with water, with paint, with mud—those swirly swirls and swings and trees.

And now there was a new cow, and of course there is no comparison really between a child and a cow except that both, like the beagle, had found their way to John and Marta's, whether by accident or intention, and John and Marta, in their quiet way, accepted these additions.

The three foundlings—beagle, boy, and cow—formed an easy alliance, glomming on to each other like old pals. The beagle would lead the way across the pasture, and Jacob would climb up on the cow and ride along as the cow followed the dog to a shady spot. There, the boy might gather rocks and pile them against the fence and either rap at them with a stick or, if there was mud nearby, paint designs on them with his finger as brush. The beagle would circle, sniffing, and the cow would munch the grass or simply stand sleepily eyeing the boy and the dog.

John and Marta might have expected—if they'd thought about it—that the boy would more likely adopt the young goats or calf as his companions, and although he did romp with them, too, he spent more time with the cow and the dog. One morning, John and Marta stood in the barn doorway, watching the boy, the beagle, and the cow, who were gathered a short distance away. John had just commented that he wished the boy would talk, that the silence was making John uneasy. He was worried that the boy might need something and be unable to communicate that need to them.

Marta had been having the same worries, but now, watching the boy, the beagle, and the cow, she noticed a pattern in the way they interacted.

"John—look at that. They're having a conversation."

John was skeptical. "The beagle and the cow?"

"The beagle, the cow, and the boy. That tapping and patting he's been doing—he has his own language there, I think, and the cow and the dog understand it. And Beagle, the way he lifts his head up and down, as if he means to bark, and the cow—she, too, moves her head up and down and murmurs in response."

"Oh, Marta, I don't think that can possibly be. That's ridic—"

"Watch."

And so they watched, and it was as Marta said. The boy

tapped on the fence, the dog barked in silence, flapping his mouth open and closed, and the cow swung her head left and right, up and down, and murmured, *Mmmm, mmmoo, mmm.* The boy tapped the cow's nose and the beagle's nose, the dog flapped his jaws, and the cow murmured, *Mmmm, mmmoo, mmm.*

"We have been so stupid!" Marta said. "All the while the boy has been 'talking' to us, and we never even knew it."

14

As John and Marta paid closer attention to the boy's tapping and patting, they quickly noticed patterns they had overlooked. There was a distinct rhythm to the way he greeted each of them:

tap-TAP-TAP-tap

and the way he greeted the dog

tap-tap-TAP

and the cow

tap-tap-TAP-TAP

and the bedtime tapping

tap-TAP-TAP-tap-tap-tap

and the after-meals tapping

TAP-tap TAP-tap.

* * *

"He's talking all day long, John!"

Gradually, they imitated his taps, so that they greeted him the way he greeted them, and they began and ended meals the way he did. The first few times, the boy reacted with his silent laugh, his shoulders bobbing up and down. But when he tapped more earnestly at other times, they did not know how to respond, and the boy seemed disappointed. They might guess what he was asking or saying, but they couldn't merely repeat the same taps in reply.

"If we teach the boy to read and write, Marta, that will solve everything, won't it? He can write down what he wants to say."

Marta wasn't completely convinced that the boy was unable to talk. She still wondered if he just was not ready to talk to them, or if he needed to recover from some horrible experience. Maybe he simply needed time. Always, too, at the back of her mind was the worry that the closer they came to know the boy and the more they loved him, the harder it would be to let him go.

15

On John's weekly trips into town for supplies, he wondered if he would discover that someone had reported a missing boy or that people were inquiring about how to find John and Marta's place. John could not understand why Jacob's family had not returned yet.

John had mentioned the boy and asked around, but no one had heard of the boy, or seemed the least bit interested, or even remembered from one week to the next that John had asked about him.

How can that be? he wondered. *How can there be a boy nobody knows about or cares about?*

One day on his visit to the general store, as John

was buying more jelly beans, Shep said, "Your wife got a sudden sweet tooth?"

"What? Oh, the candy. Ha-ha."

"Thought maybe you had a kid up there. Vernie says he thought he saw a kid riding a cow up at your place when he drove by t'other day."

"A kid—oh, sure, the one I mentioned. We're watching a kid."

"That right?" Shep said.

"Yep. Yep. Watching that kid for somebody, and that kid likes to ride cows. Imagine that."

On the far side of the store were shelves that carried used items. You might find bowls or pots or twine or rulers or bent spoons on those shelves. As John turned to go, he saw an old guitar on the floor, propped up against the shelves.

"Are you playing that or selling it?" John asked.

"The gitt-ur? That old thing? Naw, somebody left it here in trade for a couple of pots. You interested? I'll trade it to you for that jacket you're wearin'."

As John drove home, he could hardly contain himself.

Wait till the boy sees this guitar! I can hardly wait to see that face of his!

16

When John presented the guitar to Jacob, the boy took a step backward, placing his hands against his chest. He looked from John to Marta to the guitar.

"For you," John said.

The boy took another step backward.

"It's a present," Marta said. "For you."

"It's a guitar," John added. "Have you never seen a guitar?"

"It makes music," Marta said. "Listen. Show him, John."

"Haven't played one in a while," John said. He fingered a few chords, strumming a simple tune.

The boy reached out to touch the instrument.

"You hold it like this," John said, placing the guitar in the boy's arms. "Here, try this chord. Your fingers like this, that's right, and this hand, that's right, and then you can switch to this . . ."

And that was the only instruction he gave the boy, for once it was in his arms, the boy's fingers moved along the strings, slowly and tentatively at first, and then with more eagerness, and then he sat with it for hours, exploring its possibilities, and by nightfall he was already making music. It sounded like nothing else Marta or John had heard. It was as if he were re-creating the sounds of the forest and the dawn and the mountains, all rolled together. The sounds moved John and Marta greatly. One minute they would be smiling and soon after they were close to tears. It was as if the boy had control of their minds and bodies.

17

Twice a week John drove farther afield to towns small and large, sifting through gossip and local papers. What he was discovering was that boys were as likely to go missing as cows were.

"Georgia's boy run off, but came home with his tail between his legs."

"My cow broke right through the new fence."

"Carl's kid—that one with the hair—he was gone for four days and you know where they found him? In the hayloft over at Aggie's place."

"My prize Blackie cow, you seen her, right? Gone for two days, comes home with a big smile on her face."

***

MISSING: 12-year-old boy, mean as a stick. You can keep him.

MISSING: Pretty brown cow, answers to Betty.

FOUND: 12-year-old boy, mean as a stick. Come get him.

FOUND: Brown cow, not so pretty.

All the boys and cows that were lost seemed to turn up again, though, unlike the boy at John and Marta's, who had been found, but oddly, wasn't lost.

In all the time he had been at John and Marta's, the boy hadn't seemed afraid, didn't seem to miss anyone, slept soundly, and ate heartily.

"It's like he was dropped right out of the sky," John told Marta.

18

Although John was as impressed as Marta was with Jacob's talents, he was beginning to worry that the boy wasn't learning any "boy things," and he said as much to Marta.

"What are you talking about?" she said. "What kind of boy things? He rides a *cow*, doesn't he?"

"True. That's good, I guess."

"What else do you want him to do? Chop down a tree? Burn up the barn?"

"I don't know—get a little dirty, I guess."

"For heaven's sake, John, he gets dirty. I ought to know. I'm the one trying to get the dirt out of his—and your—clothes."

Still, John was bothered. So one day he took Jacob and the beagle and two fishing rods with him to the creek. His plan was to show the boy how to dig for bait and bait a hook and catch a fish.

Along the way, Jacob snatched a maple leaf and folded it into the shape of a bird. He picked up a stick and drummed it on tree trunks. He bobbed and jigged along the path with the beagle by his side. At a puddle, he stopped to trawl his fingers through the muck at the bottom and painted his arms with stripes of mud. At the edge of the creek he gathered a pile of stones and rocks and then threw them into the water with a rhythmic *plip-plop-plop-plip*.

When John dug up an earthworm and reached for his rod and hook, Jacob put his palm out, as if asking for the worm, and once he had it, he reburied it.

"But—that's our bait," John said.

Jacob tapped lightly on John's arm, *tap-tap-tap-TAP*, and returned to gathering more stones. He dug a trench along the creek bank and lined it with stones and packed the sides with mud. John watched as the boy collected twigs and leaves and built a strange sort of elfin bridge over the trench. Then Jacob climbed up on a boulder and jumped into the creek with all his clothes on. He splashed and laughed his silent laugh and then climbed back up on the rock and jumped again and again into the water. He crawled back up the muddy bank and took John's hand and beckoned the beagle, inviting them to join him.

Marta took one look at the wet, muddy man, boy, and dog as they returned to the house. "Well, John," she said. "Is he dirty enough for you?"

19

More weeks passed.

"Why doesn't anyone know about this boy?" John asked.

"We need to get him some clothes. He's looking shabby."

"Did you hear me, Marta? Why doesn't anyone—"

"I heard you. I don't know the answer to your question, but I do know that the boy needs some clothes."

They drove to the nearest town with a clothing store, some thirty miles away.

At the counter, the clerk glanced down at the boy and said, "What a quiet lad you are. What's your name?"

The boy smiled up at her.

"Cat got your tongue?"

"He's shy," John said.

"How old are you?" the clerk asked the boy.

The boy tilted his head and blinked.

"Seven—" Marta said.

"Six—" John said.

"Oops."

The clerk winked at Marta. "I know—my husband can never keep track of our kids' ages either."

The boy had twisted around to look at a woman and a young girl standing in line behind them. The boy put his hand up, palm toward the girl, and the girl raised her own palm and tapped his. The boy waggled his arms in a silly way. The girl did the same.

"Kids," the woman said to Marta. "Crazy kids."

The boy knocked his knees together and the girl did the same.

Marta felt such pride. "Yes!" she said. "Crazy kids!"

20

In the middle of fixing dinner, Marta said, "John, the boy needs to be around other kids."

"I know it, but how are we going to do that?"

"He needs a friend his age."

"He's got friends—the dog, the cow—"

"John!"

"I know, I know. I'll go nose around. See what I can come up with."

He went to town and came home with a present for the boy.

"But, John, what about the friend? Did you find him a friend?"

"No, but look at these—I traded that old hat of mine for these."

It was a used painting set: ten dimpled watercolor cubes, a frayed brush, and a pad of yellowed paper.

The boy touched each colored cube lightly, as if they were as fragile as a butterfly's wings. Marta brought him a cup of water and showed him how to dip the brush in the water and then swirl it on the paint cube. The boy leaned forward, grasping the brush, swirling it over the red, and sweeping an arc across the paper. He bent close to the paper, his hand moving deftly. He filled up an entire sheet trying every color, blending them, dotting and swishing the brush as if his hand was made to do exactly what it was doing.

He looked up at Marta and John and then at the next blank sheet of paper.

"Sure," John said. "Go right ahead."

The boy painted all afternoon. He painted until dark. He painted all the next day and the next and the next until the cubes were worn down and all the paper had been used. What started as swirly shapes quickly evolved into recognizable animals—cows, dogs, goats—and flowers and trees, cabins and barns and bridges. But the scenes were unusual: dogs stood on top of cows, flowers grew out of chimneys, bridges connected houses, barns roosted in treetops.

"Where does he come up with this stuff?" John asked.

"I don't know. I think he's a genius."

21

"Marta, we need to ask again about the boy."

"He needs to be around some kids his own age—"

"Marta—"

"—not all day, but now and then."

John went to town. This time, when he stopped at the sheriff's office, the sheriff came in while John was studying the bulletin board for new notices.

"You looking for something?" the sheriff said. He was a stocky, muscular man, his shirt tight across his chest. He had a habit of rubbing his thumb across his badge, as if to remind people exactly who he was.

"I was wondering something."

"Is that right?"

"A cow wandered onto our property and I've been waiting for someone to claim her, but no one has."

"Is that right?"

"I don't see any notices here about missing cows—"

The sheriff rubbed his thumb across his badge.

"—but if someone claims it, how do I know it really belongs to that someone?"

The sheriff looked from John to the receptionist, Darlene, and back again. "Would you be suggesting that someone might lie about owning that cow?" He aimed a finger at John's face.

"I was just wondering—let's say a couple weeks go by and nobody claims that cow, and I'm just looking after it, right? I'm not stealing it. And somebody comes along and says it's his cow—"

"Yeah, so?"

"I wouldn't be accused of stealing that cow, would I?"

"Did you steal it?"

"No! Like I said—"

"Then what are you so worried about?"

"I was just wondering, what if someone *said* I stole it?"

"Well, now, if you didn't steal it, they'd be lying. And if you did steal it, well, then—"

"I *didn't* steal it."

"Then what's the problem?"

"Should I have reported it? That cow, I mean? And how would I do that?"

"How would you do what?"

"Report it, report the cow."

"You wanna report a cow?" The sheriff turned to his receptionist. "Now that's a new one. He wants to report a cow. Ha-ha. That's a new one all right. Ha-ha-ha."

John thought, *If they don't understand about a cow, how are they going to understand about the boy?*

John left the sheriff's office and stopped at the general store, where he traded in a leather belt for a sack of jelly beans and a harmonica.

22

John and Marta stood at the barn doors listening to the boy play the harmonica to his audience: the cow, the beagle, and the goats. The cow rested her head on the top fence rail, the beagle lay on the ground between the cow's forefeet, and the baby goats were uncharacteristically still, leaning against each other, gazing at the boy. It was a slow, hypnotic tune he played.

"We've got to ask him some questions, Marta."

"But we've tried, and he seems so far away when we ask, as if he doesn't understand the simplest things, and yet—"

"—and yet other times, he seems so capable—"

"—and smart, but—"

"—quiet, very quiet."

They tried to find out how old he was, but he didn't seem to know. They asked if he had any brothers or sisters, but he merely shrugged in reply. They asked if it was his parents who left him on the porch, but he shrugged again.

"Do you even *have* any parents?" John asked.

"John, shh!"

"Well, does he or not? Jacob? Do you have any parents? Mother? Father?"

Jacob rested his chin in his hand, elbow propped on the table. He looked sleepy.

"Is someone coming to get you?" John pressed.

Jacob looked around the room, as if the answer might be there.

"Do you *want* someone to come get you?"

"John!"

"Well, I'm just asking. Do you, Jacob? Do you *want* someone to come get you?"

The boy yawned.

"What is the *matter* with him? Can't answer a simple question."

"John! Stop that. Maybe it's not such a simple question, maybe—oh, now see what you've done—"

A tear slipped down the boy's cheek.

"Now, look," Marta said, springing to the boy's side. "We've hurt his feelings."

"How did we do *that*?"

"Kids are sensitive. You ought to know that. You're a great big kid yourself."

23

"He doesn't know how to read or write. When do kids learn that, Marta?"

"I don't remember. Five? Six?"

"If we could teach him how to read and write, he could answer our questions. Try, Marta. Try to teach him."

"Me? How do you teach someone to read?"

She tried her best, but teaching reading and writing did not come naturally to Marta, and no matter how hard she tried, Jacob did not seem to catch on. If she asked him to copy the letter *A*, the boy made a scribble. If she asked him to copy the letter *B*, he drew something more like a *Q*. If she asked him to copy *s-a-t*, the boy drew a chicken.

"I think he's a lot better at painting and drawing and making music than he is ever going to be at reading and writing," Marta said.

"Is that a bad thing or a good thing?"

"Of course it's a bad thing. Isn't it, John?"

"Try some more."

Marta felt as if her hair were on fire. The pressure! The whirring of her brain. The letters whizzing around.

24

One day, John, Marta, and Jacob returned to the town where they'd bought Jacob's clothes. In a thrift shop, Jacob wandered to the back, picked up a pair of drumsticks, and rapped on the nearby drum. "That there boy has talent," the shopkeeper said. "Will you listen to that? How old are you, son?"

Marta answered. "Six. He's shy. Won't talk to strangers, you know."

"Is that right? What's your name, son?"

The boy rolled the drumsticks against the drum.

"Jacob," Marta said.

When John joined them, the shopkeeper said, "Been listening to this fine young man take a run at these drums. This your boy?"

Jacob turned his head ever so slightly toward John. Marta glanced down at her feet.

"Sure," John said. "Sure, he is."

"I can see the resemblance," the shopkeeper said. "You play the drums yourself?"

"No."

"Who taught him then?"

"Nobody. Will you take a couple dollars for this old drum set?"

Back at their truck, Marta elbowed John. "Did you hear what he said? He could see the resemblance between you and Jacob."

John reddened. "Sure, I heard him. Sure, I did."

Next, they visited a general store, full of everything from canned peaches to cow balm, from shovels to sheets. In a dusty corner, on a dusty shelf, they found art supplies, marked down in price.

"Lots of paper," Marta suggested, "and a few brushes and some of those watercolors, and . . ." She was happily immersed in selecting supplies when she heard someone say, "Hello, again."

When Marta and John quickly turned toward the voice, they saw that Jacob had settled himself on the floor beside a young girl. Her mother, standing beside them, said, "Our kids met—last week, was it? You were buying clothes, remember?"

"Oh," Marta said. "Of course, I remember."

The adults regarded the girl and Jacob, shoulder to shoulder, flipping through a book together.

"His name is Jacob," John offered.

"And that's Lucy. She's six. Nearly seven."

Marta cleared her throat. "So is Jacob. Six. Nearly seven. Hard to believe!"

"Oh, I know," the woman said. "Time sure whips by, doesn't it?"

"Weird," Marta said, "running into you again."

"Oh, I don't see anything *weird* about it at all! It must be fate. Maybe our children are meant to be friends. We're at that park over there"—she gestured toward the window and the park beyond—"nearly every Saturday morning if Jacob ever wants to join us."

"Oh, sure. Okay."

On their way home, John said, "Marta, that's a long way to go so that Jacob can have a friend."

"Shh," Marta said. "Ears."

"What?"

"We all have ears. Everyone in this car can hear, John."

"Well, of course we all have ears. Oh."

The next Saturday they returned to town and met Lucy and her mother at the park. The adults sat on a bench as Jacob and Lucy raced from swings to slide.

"Lucy can be a little bossy," her mother said. "I hope she doesn't do that with Jacob. He seems such a nice boy."

"Oh, he is," Marta said, but then regretting that she sounded as if she were bragging, she added, "but he can be a little bossy, too, sometimes."

John said, "Bossy? I don't think—"

Marta said, "See there, John? He's trying to get Lucy to follow him back to the swings."

"But that's just—"

"Bossy, bossy," Marta said. "But not often. Mostly he is such a sweet boy, wouldn't you say so, John?"

"Don't think you should call a boy 'sweet'—"

Lucy's mother laughed. "You two tickle me. I tell you what—I could never get Lucy's father to sit here and watch her play in a park."

John stood. "Oh, but I'm not—I mean, I don't usually—I was just keeping—if you two are fine here with the kids, I'll go on and, you know—"

"Sure!" Marta said. "You go on." To Lucy's mother, she said, "Aren't men funny? Once they become fathers—"

"Oh, I know, I know," Lucy's mother agreed.

"Well, John's not really a father."

"What do you mean?"

Marta pulled a tissue from her pocket. "Goodness, I don't know what—" She dabbed at her eyes and blew her nose. "We're just watching Jacob."

"Oh! I thought he was your boy."

"Mm."

"So tell me what happened."

"'Happened?'"

"Yes, why he doesn't speak. I've not heard a single sound out of him."

"Oh, that. We don't know."

"You don't know? Aren't you curious?"

"Well, sure, but the people—the people we're watching him for—they didn't say."

"That's a little odd, don't you think?"

"Yes," Marta admitted.

That night, after Jacob was in bed, Marta told John about the conversation with Lucy's mother.

"John, I do not know what has come over me. I feel so happy when we're around the boy, and then all of a sudden, I want to bust into tears."

"I know," John said. "I know."

25

Jacob learned to play the drums as swiftly as he had learned the guitar. He seemed to know a hundred different rhythms, and he could make the drums sound like so many different things: horses' clopping and cannons and footsteps. He could sound the beating of a heart, the beating of wings.

When he wasn't playing the drums or the guitar or riding the cow or running with the beagle, Jacob painted scenes of the pasture, the house, the animals. He painted trees and flowers and birds. Sometimes he painted explosions of color and line, unlike anything Marta and John had ever seen before.

"Marta, I still think he needs to be learning some

other things," John said.

"Like what?"

"Chores."

"Fine, then," Marta said. "Show him how to do some chores."

And so John showed Jacob how to feed the cows and goats. "Each day, you do this. I'm counting on you, Jacob. Understand?"

Jacob nodded, just once, which was his way, and some days he remembered to feed them and some days he didn't.

"How come he doesn't remember, Marta? How come I have to keep reminding him? Should I be hollering at him?"

"Oh, no, you shouldn't do *that*."

"Well, that's what *my* father did when I forgot to do something."

"And did his hollering help you remember?"

"No."

"Well, then—"

"But his whippin' did. Should I whip the boy?"

"Oh, *no*, John, you wouldn't—"

"No, no, I couldn't."

Another day, John asked Marta what else he should be teaching the boy.

"How to use a hammer and saw and all," Marta suggested.

That afternoon, John asked Jacob to follow him down the drive. "Going to mend the fence, boy. You could help with this." The beagle followed the boy. John carried a hammer, pliers, and a sack of nails. "You could—"

John stopped abruptly. The sheriff's car was turning off the road into the long dirt drive.

"Jacob—run on up to the house, quick, *now*, go on, fast as you can, it's okay, go on—"

Jacob took off for the house, with the beagle trailing him.

The sheriff pulled up alongside John, dirt swirling up in John's face. The sheriff leaned out the window.

"Howdy there."

"Howdy, Sheriff. What can I do for you?"

The sheriff lifted his hat, smoothed his hair, and replaced the hat on his head. "About a cow. Old man Krankins lost his cow—he says it's an old Angus. That the kind you found?"

"No, sir, it's not, sorry to say."

"You're sure about that?"

"Sure as sure can be. The one that ended up here ain't no Angus, not by a long stretch. Heck, it's got—"

"Okay, then, sorry to trouble you." The sheriff rubbed his hand over his badge.

"No trouble. No trouble at all, Sheriff."

The sheriff turned his car around, but stopped again and leaned out the window. "Was that a boy I saw running up there?"

"Yep. We're watching him."

"That right? He must like it here."

"Yep. I guess he does."

"That the boy that rides cows?"

"Yep. That's the one."

"Well, I'll be going now. You let me know if you see Krankins's old Angus cow."

"I will. Sure, I will."

26

Marta and John watched Jacob riding the cow across the pasture, trailed by the beagle.

"That's some boy," John said.

"I know it."

"He's not your usual sort of boy, is he?"

"Well, I don't know what a usual sort of boy is, to tell you the truth."

"All that music and art stuff he does, how does he know how to do that? And is that good for him?"

Marta didn't answer. Sometimes John needed to toss questions out into the air, but he didn't always expect an answer. It had taken her a long time to learn that about him, but when she did, she was vastly relieved. It had been exhausting trying to answer all his questions. Sometimes she made up answers just so she wouldn't have to say "I don't know" one more time.

"What about school?" John asked. "That's going to start up soon. What are we going to do then? What if the sheriff comes back? What about the people? Are they coming back or not? We can't keep the boy forever, can we?"

After Jacob and Lucy had played together on the playground the previous week, Lucy's mother had suggested they meet regularly, every Saturday. Marta had agreed before checking with John.

"You should have checked with me, Marta. I'm not sure we should be getting so cozy with—"

"Oh, John, shoot. The boy has to have a friend— beyond a cow and a dog and a couple goats. He needs a *human* friend. What possible harm could there be?"

On the third Saturday, Lucy's mother asked, "Do you watch Jacob every weekend?"

"For the time being, yes."

And then Lucy's mother asked where Jacob went to school. "Lucy's over here at Shady Vale Elementary. Second grade next year. Jacob, too?"

"Too?"

"Second grade?"

"Oh, no, no. I mean, he might be, but—"

"Oh, I'm sorry. Is it because of him being, you know, mute, that—"

"Mute?" *Is that what people would call Jacob?* Marta wondered. *People who did not even know him?*

"Isn't that what—oh, I'm so sorry—have I upset you?"

Marta wanted to grab Jacob and race back to the truck, where John would be waiting. She wanted to speed away. But she could not. Instead, she said, "No, no, not at all. Sometimes, well, it is so sensitive, you know—"

"His parents? They're sensitive about it?"

"Well—"

"Who *are* his parents? Relatives of yours?"

"No—"

"Shh, shh, I'm sorry. I think I've been a little too nosy. Look, Jacob's showing Lucy how to use those twigs like drumsticks. How cute is *that*?"

And now, nearly a week later, Marta was dreading their Saturday outing, dreading the questions that might surprise her.

"John," she said, as they watched Jacob lean forward on the cow, resting his head against the cow's neck, "September will be here before we know it. Maybe we should find out about school."

John felt his feet sinking into the ground. He was going to be swallowed up. Whenever Marta said, "Maybe we should," what she really meant was "Maybe *you* should." And he did not know the first thing about putting a child in school.

27

The boy found a snake. It was small and green and narrow, weaving swiftly through the tall grass. Jacob scooped it up and studied it, head to tail. The snake curled around his wrist and lifted its head, as if it, too, were studying the creature who held it.

The beagle backed away, flapping his silent mouth, scolding the snake.

Marta was sweeping the porch when Jacob approached.

"What's that you have—oh—well, now—" She stepped back. "That appears to be a—well, well—"

The snake was comfortably coiled around Jacob's wrist and in his palm.

"John," Marta called. "John, come see what—there, there, ooh, my, what a nice—what an interesting—*John*!"

John beamed when he saw the boy holding the snake.

"Well, lookee there, you caught a little garter snake. Isn't he something?"

"John, I think you and Jacob might want to take that—out—somewhere—else."

"Oh, sure," he said.

Later that day, when the boy was riding the cow, John said, "How about that boy, Marta? He caught a snake. I think he's going to be just fine."

"Well, goody good, but I want you to know one thing, John. I *hate* snakes. I hate the sight of them, I hate the very thought of them, and no boy of mine is bringing any snakes in this house."

"Sure, sure, I understand," John said. "But how about that? He caught a snake! And he wasn't even afraid."

"*Huh!* I don't see what's so miraculous about *that*."

John didn't see any point in explaining, even if he could, but he was thinking, *How about that? My boy caught a snake!*

That night a storm blew through. Winds lashed the trees, sending buckets tumbling and barn doors rattling. Chairs skidded across the back porch and roof shingles flapped and flipped.

In the morning, John and Marta surveyed the debris cluttering the yard. The wind had sheared the top off of a tall shagbark hickory tree and thrust its branches onto the roof.

"Best cut the rest of that tree down," John said. "Knew it was mostly hollow. It's a skinny thing, shouldn't be any trouble."

Marta and the boy watched from the porch as John finished sawing the base. The tree came down with a clean *swoosh* and *thud*.

Jacob's gaze fastened on something dropping out of a knothole in the newly fallen tree. He rushed forward, the beagle at his side.

"What is it?" John asked. "What's he after, Marta?"

They heard tiny cries, barely audible squeaks.

The boy nudged the beagle behind him and crouched, his arms forming a protective circle around four squirming, squealing critters.

"Well, lookee there," John said, coming to the boy's side. "Baby squirrels. Newly born, I'd say, one or two days old at most."

"Are you sure, John? They look so—I don't know—so creepy."

"They're squirrels all right. Let them be."

"But what will happen to them?"

"They're rodents. We don't need any more rodents." John moved to the upper portion of the fallen tree and began sawing off limbs.

"Come on, Jacob," Marta said, "you can help me round up the buckets and baskets that went flying last night."

She was halfway to the barn when she realized Jacob wasn't following her. He was scooping up dirt and leaves and nudging the baby squirrels into a roughly fashioned nest in his hands. After he carried his bundle to the hollow stump and gently set them inside, Jacob moved to the shade of another tree on the far side of the house. From there he could watch over the stump.

The boy didn't come in to dinner.

"He's still watching that old stump," John said. "I tried to get him to come in, but he looked so worried, I thought I'd better leave him. I wish I knew what he was thinking, Marta."

"He's probably wondering if the mother will come back," she said, and as soon as she said that, she felt something clump in her chest.

28

One day the boy cried.

He had fed the animals and then sat on the fence playing his guitar.

"It's so mournful," Marta said.

"How does he know these songs?"

"I think he makes them up as he goes."

"How does a person *do* that, Marta? I can't hardly fathom it."

"Usually he plays sweeter songs. This one's so sad. Is *he* sad?"

The boy stopped playing, his hands still cradling the guitar. He bowed his head.

Marta and John went to the boy's side and saw that

he was crying.

"What's wrong?" Marta asked, putting an arm around his shoulders.

John knelt in front of the boy. "Did something happen?"

The boy gestured to the hollow stump where he had left the baby squirrels.

John walked over to the stump, knelt, and peered inside. "They're gone. The babies are gone."

The boy tapped his chest.

"The mother came back for them?"

The boy nodded.

"Well, that's good then, isn't it, honey?"

The boy's thumb slid across the strings. He looked at the sky and back down at the ground, as if he weren't sure of the answer to her question.

After the boy was asleep that evening, Marta said, "John, I can hardly stand it. That boy must miss his mother and we are being entirely selfish and we have to find her."

"I know it."

"What were we thinking? How could we —"

"He seemed so happy here, though."

"He did, he did. And they *asked* us to watch him."

"They *said* they'd be back."

* * *

The next morning, they saw the boy racing in the yard with the dog. They saw him climb the fence and slide onto the cow's back, laughing his silent laugh. They saw him slide off the cow onto the grass and roll down the hill with the dog and the goats chasing after him. They saw him dip a brush into the paint can and paint a glorious blue tree shading a red goat. They heard him tapping a lively beat on the drums. They saw him hug the dog and accept the dog's slobbery licks on his face.

"See?" Marta said. "He *is* happy."

"I'm feeling mighty confused, Marta."

29

John was in the sheriff's office.

"You find old man Krankins's cow?" the sheriff asked.

"No, that's not why I've come."

"You lose somethin'?"

"No."

The sheriff's thumb slid across his badge, shining it. "Well, then?"

And so John told him about the boy, about how the boy had appeared on their porch and how they'd become protective of him and fond of him.

The sheriff pointed a finger at John. "So, are you saying you lied to me?"

"Well, sir, I did try to—"

"You lied to me. You said you were watching the boy for someone."

"Well, sir, technically we are. We just don't know who that someone is."

"And you didn't bother to report this?"

"Well, sir, I did *try*. You may recall I came here to inquire about a missing boy."

"But you didn't tell me the whole truth, did you?"

"No, sir. Not precisely. I probably should've asked about missing *parents*."

"You could be locked up for this, you know that?"

"No, sir."

"I'm *telling* you: you could be locked up for this."

John took a step back. "Do you mean to tell me that protecting a child and feeding him and caring for him is a crime?"

The sheriff again pointed at John. "It is if you don't have permission. It is if nobody knows where that child is."

"He had a note, see?"

Plees taik kair of Jacob.
He is a ~~god~~ good boy.
Wil be bak wen we can.

The sheriff studied the note. "How do I know you didn't write this note yourself?"

"What? Look, I didn't write the note. We don't know who did write it. We figured they'd be back later that day, or the next day, or—"

"And nobody knew where this boy was?"

"What? The people knew—the people who left him. And maybe they told other people. And *we* knew where he was. My wife and I knew."

"Don't be getting clever with me."

"No, sir. No, sir, I won't."

"So why did you come in here today?"

"I suppose we ought to try to find the boy's family."

"You tired of the boy, is that it? Ready to be rid of him?"

"No, sir. No, no. My wife—she'd be heartbroken to give him up—but we want to do the right thing by the boy."

"And you expect me to believe that you didn't snatch this boy from somebody's yard? This boy just appeared on your porch one morning?"

"It's the truth."

The sheriff's receptionist, Darlene, came in from the back room.

"What's the truth?" she asked.

30

They were all in the barn: Marta, John, Jacob, and the sheriff.

Marta's heart was thumping in her chest; John's tongue felt as dry as if he'd licked sand.

The boy was sitting on a hay bale, drumming on a pail with two sticks. The beagle was curled at his feet.

"So this is the boy?" the sheriff asked. "The one that just appeared one day?"

Marta wanted to grab the boy and flee. She wanted to thunk the sheriff on the head. She wanted to scream.

"Let's have a look at him," the sheriff said. "Come here, boy."

The boy kept drumming, engrossed in his work.

"Is he deaf or what?"

"No!" Marta said.

"He doesn't obey?"

"He doesn't know you, that's all, or maybe he didn't hear you because he's concentrating."

The sheriff approached the boy.

Marta slipped in front of the sheriff and knelt beside the boy. "This is the sheriff," she explained. "He wants to meet you."

"What's his name again?"

"Jacob. He doesn't speak."

"Boy!" the sheriff shouted.

"He's *not* deaf. You don't have to shout at him," Marta said, "and he has a name: Jacob."

"Yeah, you told me. Boy, look at me. How'd you get here?"

"We told you, he doesn't speak," Marta said.

"Boy, did these people snatch you and bring you here?"

"Sheriff!"

"Did they, boy?"

The boy drummed on.

"Are they keeping you penned up here in the barn?"

"Sheriff!"

"Doesn't he even nod 'yes' or 'no'?"

"Sure, he does."

"Then why isn't he doing that? Boy, did somebody else bring you here? Did somebody drop you off?"

The beat of the tin drums was lively. The beagle thumped his tail.

"Where you from, boy? Come on, say something."

"He *doesn't speak*, Sheriff."

"So you said. Maybe you threatened him, told him not to talk."

Marta stood. "Sheriff! We did *not* threaten him. Look at him. Does he look afraid? Does he look threatened? No, he looks content. He is happy here."

The sheriff walked around the property and checked inside the house. He saw the drums and paints and the small room that had been set up for the boy to sleep in.

"And you say he just appeared on your porch one day, is that right?"

"Yes," John said.

"Out of the blue, just like that?"

"Yes."

"Sorta like that cow that appeared one day?"

"Well, sort of, but not the same, I mean the boy wasn't tied up to the railing like the cow was. The boy was just asleep on the porch, and he had a note. The cow didn't have a note."

"Uh-huh." The sheriff tapped his boot against the railing. "And how many days has he been here?"

"Days? Well, now—let's see—I can't exactly remember—it's been more like weeks—"

"Weeks? He's been here for *weeks*?"

"Well, now, I don't exactly—"

"And you're just now getting around to reporting it?"

John sank onto a chair on the porch and pressed his hands to his face. He did not want to cry in front of the sheriff, but that's what he felt like doing. He wanted to sob like a baby.

"Sheriff, we didn't mean to get attached to him, but—"

"Okay, okay, I get it. I've got kids and grandkids. I get it."

"You do?"

"Look, it still sounds fishy to me, but the boy looks well cared for, so he can stay here for now."

It hadn't occurred to John that the sheriff might take the boy away. That thought filled John with such dread that he thought he'd be sick all over the sheriff's feet.

"Sheriff, you wouldn't, you couldn't just take—"

"This boy isn't yours."

"But, you couldn't just take—"

"I *am* the *law.*" The sheriff tapped his badge and returned to his car. "I'll be doing some checking around. I'll let you know if I find out anything."

31

John and Marta were rattled with worry. In front of the boy, they tried to remain calm and cheerful, as usual, but at night they lay awake.

"I shouldn't have gone to the sheriff," John said.

"You had to do that, sooner or later."

"I wish I hadn't gone. I didn't like his tone, did you?"

"No. He acted as if we were criminals."

"As if we had stolen the boy."

"As if we were keeping him here against his will."

"The nerve!"

The next morning, the boy started a new painting

in the barn. He had already filled the lower section of one side of the barn with a wide landscape: blue trees and red paths and purple animals and blue and red and purple swirls and bubbles in the air. He'd found some black paint and created an enormous black cloud hovering over the scene.

Marta came running into the barn. "John! John!"

"What? What's wrong? Is it the sheriff?"

"No, no. I just realized—it just came to me—look—" She stood beside him, lowering her voice and indicating the painted scene. "Maybe *that's* where he's from."

"What? You think he's painting it?"

"Why didn't we ever think of that?"

"But, Marta—what—you think he's from a blue forest or something?"

"No, don't be silly."

They watched the boy begin a new scene: it looked like a creek.

Marta tapped the boy's shoulder and turned him toward the other wall with its completed scene. "Do you know that place?" she asked.

The boy regarded the painting.

"Is that where you came from?"

The boy scratched the back of his neck.

90

"Is that your—home?"

The boy scratched his knee.

"Marta, maybe he doesn't remember—"

"How could he not remember?"

"Well, you know, kids might not—"

"How could he paint it if he didn't remember it?"

That night, Marta suggested a plan. "We'll go exploring."

"We will?"

"All three of us. See this map? See this circle? We'll get in the truck and cover all this area."

"And we'll be looking for what exactly?"

"For that scene he painted."

"For blue trees and purple animals and red creek?"

"Don't be silly, John."

32

And so, the next morning they set off, the three of them in the truck, along with the beagle, who leaped in at the last minute and snuggled by the boy's feet. They planned to wander along the back roads for a few hours, looking for the scene on the wall of the barn.

They turned down narrow roads they had not traveled before; they rolled through small towns with dilapidated stores and abandoned gas stations. They passed neglected shacks and derelict buildings and cast-off, rusty vehicles and appliances. They passed many barns, some small and rustic, and some larger, older ones with sunken roofs and tilting frames.

The first time they came to a wooded area bordered by a creek, John slowed the truck and Marta caught her breath, sat back in her seat, and gripped the door handle. The boy was looking at a nearby house. He pointed to the porch.

"What? No, oh no. What?" Marta said. "Is it—?"

The boy smiled and waved his hand at the porch.

"Is it—do you know that place?"

But the boy had already turned away and was reaching for the dog, rubbing his head.

John said, "Look there—see that? It's probably just those chickens he was waving at."

"Oh. Thank goodness. I mean—"

"I know," John said. "I know."

And on they drove through the countryside, through small towns, past several pastures and creeks, and none of them seemed especially familiar to Jacob.

When they returned home that afternoon, and the boy had run up to the pasture to greet the cows and goats, Marta said, "Let's have a big dinner tonight. I'm starved! Let's have fried chicken and mashed potatoes and green beans with bacon and—oh!—I'll make a pie—we haven't had apple pie in ages. It feels so good to be back home today, doesn't it, John? Doesn't it feel good to be home?"

"Yes, it does."

33

On Saturday, they drove to the park where they usually met Lucy and her mother. Marta had resolved that she was going to tell Lucy's mother the whole truth about the boy.

"It will be good to get it out in the open," she told John.

"If you think so."

Lucy and Jacob were by now fast friends, attached to each other as if they'd known each other for years. Lucy would run up to him and grab his hand and off they would go, dashing to the swings or slide or climbing bars.

"She's so motherly," Lucy's mother said. "Look how

she holds Jacob's hand. Cute."

"Yes, well . . ."

"You really should come to our house sometime—just leave Jacob for a day. They would have such fun. Would that be okay with, you know, his family?"

"Ah, well . . ."

"Or, if you'd rather, I could bring Lucy to your house."

"There's something I want to tell you first," Marta said. Her hands fluttered helplessly. She looked around for John, but he had already returned to the truck.

"Sure, what is it? Is something wrong?"

"No, no, not wrong." Feeling as if she could not turn back, Marta barreled on ahead, telling Lucy's mom about finding the boy on the porch and not knowing where he had come from or who had left him.

Lucy's mother sat up straight. "You *found* him on your porch? You don't know who left him? You don't know when they're coming back?"

"That's right."

"But how strange, how odd. That's a bit creepy, don't you think?"

"Creepy? Well, I wouldn't say that—"

"But what are you going to do?"

"Try to find his family."

"But if you do—have you thought about that? What happens if you do find them?"

"I don't know."

"There, there. Shh." She put a protective arm around Marta. "Shh. What a strange, strange thing. Shh."

34

Again they drove out into the surrounding countryside, this time with renewed urgency and renewed dread.

"John, I just have to know—"

"Yes—"

"—where he came from, how he ended up here, what his life was like, how anyone could part with him—if anyone is coming back for him—"

They drove up and down the hills, along the winding roads, past miles and miles of dense trees and small streams.

"So beautiful here," Marta said. She tapped the boy's arm. "Beautiful, don't you think?"

The boy gazed out the window and tapped his chest.

Marta looked into the boy's eyes. "You understand so much, don't you?"

The boy nodded.

"I wish I knew what was in your head. I wish I knew what you were thinking all the time."

At the crest of a hill, John pulled over. "Let's walk a bit," he said. "Too nice a day to be cooped up inside this truck."

And so they walked along a trail that led from the top of the hill to a creek below. The boy and the beagle ran ahead, dashing off the path from time to time and then circling back again.

"This is nice," Marta said.

"Yes," John agreed.

"I wish it could be like this always."

Over the next two weeks, they drove out into new areas, and each time, they stopped the truck to walk a scenic path or explore a creek. On one such day, they parked near a public beach at a small lake, well concealed by dense woods. From the beach they tossed stones into the water and dug in the sand. The beagle chased the boy up and down the deserted, narrow beach. After a picnic, they followed a path through the trees and ate from blackberry bushes.

The dog found a ragged red rubber ball and brought it to the boy's feet. The boy threw the ball, the dog retrieved it and brought it back, enjoying the game. On one throw, the ball bounced off the path into the leaves, and when the dog returned, he brought a dirty, sodden child's shoe.

"Aw, some poor child has lost his shoe," Marta said.

"Leave it," John said. "It's filthy."

The boy seemed intrigued by the shoe, turning it this way and that. He sat down on the ground and took off his own shoe and tried to wedge his foot into the dirty shoe.

"What—? What are you—?"

"Leave it," John repeated. "Don't be silly. It's filthy and it's too small anyway. Can't you see that?"

But the boy tried again to force his foot into the shoe.

"Cut that out," John said. He knelt to put the boy's own shoe back on and tossed the dirty shoe to the side of the trail.

They had barely moved on when the boy returned to reclaim the shoe, clutching it in his hand.

"Why?" Marta asked. "Why do you want that old shoe?"

The boy tapped his foot and then raced on.

"Funny kid," Marta said. "Wanting that old shoe."

"Yeah. Funny kid," John agreed.

35

The boy did not want to part with the shoe. He carried it with him all that day, took it to bed with him that night, and toted it around all the next day. While he painted on the barn wall, the shoe rested on a stool beside him. When the beagle snatched the shoe, the boy gently removed it from the dog's mouth and wedged it in his pocket.

It was a flimsy canvas shoe, the sort a child might wear in the summer, its sole worn, the canvas stained with mud and mold. It took some convincing for the boy to allow Marta to wash it. He stood by the tin tub while it soaked. He took the stiff brush from Marta and scrubbed the shoe, rinsed it, and pegged it to the line to dry.

He checked on the shoe so often that John said, "It's just a shoe. It's not going anywhere."

The boy seemed startled. He tapped rapidly on John's arm, an urgent and insistent message.

"What? What?"

The boy gave John a look that he had not seen before. Was it disappointment? Was the boy disappointed in John?

"Okay, okay," John said. "It's *not* just any old shoe."

To Marta, later, John said, "That shoe is bothering me."

"Don't be silly, John. It's just a *shoe*."

The next day they returned to the spot where they'd found the shoe. It had rained the night before and the earth was dark, the leaves still dripping here and there. The sky was overcast, the lake flat and gray.

Again, the boy and the beagle ran ahead. The boy had insisted on carrying a knapsack with the shoe inside.

"I thought we were going to try different places each time," Marta said.

"I know, but there was something about this spot—it's nice here, don't you think?"

"If it's so nice, why do you look so worried?"

"Worried? I'm not worried."

The boy and the beagle roamed in and out of the trees, on and off the path. Before they reached the beach, the boy returned to their sides, holding aloft the shoe, wet and stained with mud.

"You got it dirty again? Why'd you do that?" John asked.

The boy shrugged the knapsack off his shoulder, opened it, and retrieved the clean shoe. He held it next to the dirty one.

"The other shoe!" Marta said.

John leaned in for a closer look. "What do you know! You found the other one."

The boy held the shoes close to his chest. Then he knelt, and with a stick, he drew in the dirt a figure of a child. Next to it, he drew a taller child. He placed the found shoes at the feet of the first, smaller figure. He sat down, took off his own shoes, and placed them at the feet of the taller child.

"I don't get it," John said. "What's he trying to tell us?"

The boy thought a minute. Then he scratched out the figures and began again. He drew a child in the dirt. At the child's feet, he placed the found shoes.

"You did that already," John said.

Then the boy made the same figure bigger. He

elongated the body, the arms, the legs. He made the feet larger. Now he removed the found shoes and placed his own shoes at the feet of the drawing.

"The boy grew!" Marta said. "His feet grew. He needed larger shoes, right?"

"Well, of course," John said. "If your feet grow, you need—"

"Oh—" Marta knelt beside the boy and lifted the found shoes. "Are these *your* shoes?"

The boy nodded, and as he did so, he exhaled deeply, as if he were releasing volumes of trapped air.

36

On the day the boy found the second shoe, after
they'd eaten their sandwiches at the beach and
after the boy and the beagle had run through the paths,
John steered the truck down a road that, he guessed,
would lead them around the far side of the lake. It
would be a longer route home, but the sun had come
out and the air was fresh, a perfect day for a drive along
a country road.

It was on this day that the boy, who had been
studying the second shoe as he sat between John and
Marta, with the beagle at his feet, suddenly slapped the
shoe against the dashboard. He lunged for the window
at Marta's side and leaned out, his head turning this

way and that.

Marta grasped the boy tightly. "Don't do that! Whatever are you—stop—you're going to fall out! John, stop this truck!"

John pulled to the side of the road and had barely stopped the truck when the boy jumped out, tugging at Marta's sleeve. The beagle, picking up on the boy's agitation, ran in circles around the trio, shaking its head, pawing at the boy's legs.

"What happened?" John asked. "Did something bite him? Did he cut himself? What's the—"

Marta was standing as still as a fence post. John followed her gaze. In the distance was a shabby trailer surrounded by rusted bits of metal. At one end was a tall, narrow tree, its trunk painted blue, and from it hung a swing.

The boy gripped Marta's hand as she and John remained standing by the side of the road, unable to move.

"Do you know this place, Jacob?" Marta asked. "Do you—why, you're *trembling*."

The boy backed toward the truck.

"John, let's go. I don't like this. Jacob doesn't like this—"

"Get in the truck. Wait for me," John said, and he headed off toward the trailer to investigate.

In the truck, Jacob slipped to the floor and hid his head in his hands. Marta locked the doors and strained to follow John's movements.

The trailer was abandoned, inhabited only by startled squirrels. Leaves and dirt and tattered bits of clothing littered the damp, dark rooms, cobwebs clouded the windows, and dirty pots filled the sink. John retrieved a worn, soiled stuffed toy—a rabbit—and returned to the truck.

When John offered Jacob the stuffed animal, the boy scowled, snatched the rabbit, and threw it out the window. With his fists, he pounded on the dashboard and shook his head back and forth. John and Marta had never seen him so agitated.

And so they drove home, silent and shaken.

They remained silent as they walked up to the pasture and barn to feed the animals. The cows and the goats murmured greetings and swung their heads this way and that, puzzled. The beagle rubbed up against each of the animals, communicating his own confusion.

Something is different, the dog seemed to be saying. That knowledge circulated among the animals.

Something is different. Something has changed.

* * *

That night, John said to his wife, "The sheriff might be able to investigate more."

Marta did not answer. Instead, she got up and went to check on the boy, who was sound asleep, with the beagle curled beside him.

37

They considered moving.

They'd take Jacob, of course, and the dog, but they'd sell the other animals and the house and make a new start somewhere else.

"No one would be asking questions about the boy. They would assume he belonged to us—"

"And we could just go on with our lives and everyone would be happy."

"But the people—if they came back—"

"Does it look like they're coming back?"

"No, but they might, and if they did come back, and we weren't here, then they might call the sheriff and—"

"What about a birth certificate? Isn't he going to need one of those?"

"Lots of people can't find their birth certificates."

"But—"

"But—"

Round and round they went: *Should we stay or should we go?*

38

They stayed.

And the days went on as before, and when September came, John met with the sheriff and explained that the people had not returned for the boy, and they wanted to arrange legal custody of Jacob.

"Well, now, that might take some time," the sheriff said. "Up at the county courthouse, things move as slow as a turtle in quicksand. We could get the welfare people out here, but naw, that department is a mess. You best hold on to the boy for the time being and see if those people show up, I guess, long as the boy doesn't mind being with you."

When John told the sheriff about the abandoned

trailer, the sheriff promised to investigate.

At the schoolhouse, John was told that it might be better to wait until January to see about enrolling the boy, when they were better staffed. They did not know what to do with a child who did not speak.

"But he's very talented," John said. "He can draw—"

"All kids draw."

"And music, he's very talented in music, too—"

"All parents think that about their kids."

That afternoon, John, Marta, and Jacob drove out to an orchard and picked a bushel of ripe, red apples. And while the sun was shining down on them as they munched on the fruit, and as the beagle ran in and out of the boy's legs, back at their farmhouse, several miles away, an old car pulled into the drive.

A car door slammed shut.

"Hello? Hello?"

39

As soon as John and Marta saw the old car in their drive, they sensed the dark cloud that was about to descend upon them. Jacob slid to the floor and clutched Marta's ankle.

A man leaned against the fence. He was thin and pale, in baggy, faded clothes.

"Marta, stay in the truck with Jacob," John said.

The thin man said what John and Marta had most dreaded.

"I've come for the boy."

40

"I'm his father and I've come for him," the man said.

John turned to Jacob. "Is this your father?"

Jacob nodded and then tentatively tapped at his father's arm.

"No" was his father's reply. "We're going now."

Jacob did not appear afraid of his father, but it was clear that he did not want to leave. He clung to Marta.

"But where will you take him?" Marta asked.

The man named a town three hundred miles away, where he'd found work and a place to live.

"We could keep the boy for you," John offered.

"'Keep' him? What do you mean? He's *my* boy, and I'll do the keepin'."

"I mean in case you need more time—or if it would be too hard for you to have the boy—or—"

"I can do just fine. I never said nothin' about you keepin' the boy. I never did."

"You didn't say much at all. We didn't know who you were or when—or if—you might come back."

"I said I was comin' back."

John pressed the man. "You said '*We*'. Why'd you say '*we*'? Who else—?"

"I didn't know it'd be just me. His ma—she ran off."

Jacob's head bent to his chest.

"But why here? Why us?"

"You don't remember me?" he asked John. "I worked up at Vernie Gossem's for a time—when you was working on his place."

"I—I—honestly, I don't remember—"

"Vernie said you was a good man, that you had a good wife, too."

"That's all you knew about us? And you left your boy here?"

A second car pulled in the drive.

"What's that sheriff doing here?" the man said. He crossed his arms and spit to one side.

For once, both Marta and John were relieved to see the sheriff's car.

The sheriff slid slowly out of his seat, gave his badge a firm rub, and said, "Saw a strange car up here, out-of-state plates." He eyed the man leaning against the old car.

"Says he's the boy's father," John explained.

The sheriff rested one hand on the gun in his holster. "That so?"

The man did not flinch. "Yeah, that's so. I'm his father and I've come to take him."

The sheriff rubbed his chin. "And how do we know you're telling the truth?"

"Wha—? Why, heck. Ask him. Ask the boy."

"The boy doesn't talk," the sheriff said.

"He can nod. Ask him."

So the sheriff asked Jacob if this was his father and Jacob nodded and then lowered his head again and tightened his grasp of Marta's hand.

John stepped forward. "You got any proof? Any papers?"

"Yeah," the sheriff agreed. "You got any papers?"

"Wha—?"

John said, "A real father wouldn't want me releasing his boy to just anybody, not without some sort of proof."

The man slapped the side of his car. "Proof? That's ridiculous." He kicked a tire, then spun around. "Wait a minute. Wait just a minute—"

The man unlocked the trunk, revealing a crammed jumble of clothes and boxes and bulging trash bags. He burrowed into the pile like a rat on a hunt.

The sheriff motioned for John, Marta, and the boy to step away.

"What are you looking for?" the sheriff demanded.

"Proof! I've got proof!"

"You better not be looking for any guns."

The man mumbled something as he burrowed farther into the heap. "Lucky thing I'm moving and got all my stuff with me."

The boy inched forward, curious. John and Marta exchanged a desperate look.

"Here!" the man said, backing out of the trunk with a tattered cardboard box in his hands. He fumbled through yellowed bits of paper. "There you go!" he said triumphantly, shoving a creased document toward the sheriff. "Proof enough?" He dug in his pocket. "And here's some more." He pulled out his driver's license. "To prove I'm me."

John and Marta joined the sheriff in examining the first document.

"Looks like a valid birth certificate for the boy," the sheriff said.

Marta could not remain silent. "We've given him a good home. Jacob is happy here. We can care for him—feed him and clothe him and look after him the way he should be looked after."

"Are you tellin' me I don't know how to look after my own boy? 'Cause I'm telling you it don't matter what you think. He's *my* boy."

John whirled toward the sheriff. "What can we do?"

The sheriff studied the man, the boy, the papers in his hand. "Well, now, the way I see it, you don't have much choice, sorry to say. The man is his father, and a father has a right to his boy, don't he?"

"But—"

The sheriff returned to his own car. "Don't he?" he repeated.

As Jacob trailed forlornly behind, Marta and John gathered his things. When the father saw the guitar and drums and box of paint supplies, he said, "He don't need all that and I don't have room for any of it."

Jacob clutched the guitar, refusing to release it.

"Please let him take it," Marta urged. "He's so talented."

The man snorted. "You making fun of my boy 'cause he cain't talk?"

"No, no. I meant—his drawing, his music—"

"Lord Almighty, woman, that stuff ain't going to do him any good in this world."

"May we write to him? May we see him again?"

"Sure, sure," the man said. "Sure. Look, he can take the guitar, okay? Probably won't last a week, but sure . . ."

Jacob went with his father. His head was bowed, his shoulders slumped, his feet leaden. He did not cry.

Up in the pasture, the animals sensed the change in the air. The cows hung their heads, the goats muttered sadly, and the beagle wove in and out between their legs, passing along the news.

The boy is gone, the boy is gone.

41

The boy is gone, the boy is gone.

Each morning, they heard that refrain. Each afternoon, each evening, they heard that refrain. They heard it in the farmhouse, in the pasture, in the barn.

The boy is gone, the boy is gone.

Each morning, John woke early and slipped out to the porch, and always, always, he was disappointed to see the empty chair.

The boy is gone, the boy is gone.

Marta woke in the middle of the night and went to the empty bed.

The boy is gone . . .

The beagle sniffed the farmhouse and the yard

relentlessly, curling against objects that the boy had touched.

The boy is gone . . .

John and Marta strained at the sound of cars passing on the road below. Would this one bring the boy back?

No vehicles turned into the drive.

The boy . . .

They sent cards and letters to the boy, and each day, they checked the mailbox at the end of the drive for a reply from the father, but no reply came, and after a few weeks, their own letters began coming back to them, stamped *Unable to deliver* and *No such address*.

The boy was gone.

42

At the sheriff's office, John explained that the letters had been returned.

"*Unable to deliver,*" John said.

"Is that right?"

"Yes, and *No such address.*"

"Is that right?"

"Yes. He lied to us—that man lied to us."

"Maybe he just got the address wrong. That happens, don't it?"

"We're worried about the boy. We never should have let him—"

"You didn't have much choice."

"But we never, never should have let—"

"The boy wasn't yours."

John wanted to say to the sheriff, *How do you go on with your days when the boy is gone? You wake up, your feet feel heavy, your arms feel heavy, your head is so heavy you can barely hold it up.*

But then he knew what they had to do.

They had to find the boy.

43

And so they set off for the town the father had mentioned. As they feared, there was "no such address" as the one the father had given John and Marta. It was a straggly town with one filling station, a general store, and a diner. People looked at them blankly when John and Marta asked about the young boy and his father.

"Don't know who you could be talkin' about," one waitress said. "People come in here from off the road, strangers, we don't keep track. Maybe they were here, maybe they weren't."

They described Jacob more fully; they explained about the constant tapping.

"Lots of kids tap, don't they? I got a kid who pounds on everything in sight."

John and Marta went to the nearest post office, the hospital, the school.

Nothing.

They returned home. When the sheriff said he'd had no luck investigating the trailer, John and Marta visited the property again. They spoke to the owners of the land, who said that a man and woman had rented the trailer for a few months only. Yes, they had a young boy. The owners did not know where they had come from or where they went when they left.

"Skipped out on the rent. Left in the middle of the night."

44

When the first snow fell, Marta and John boxed up the boy's things—the paints and brushes and drums that the father would not let the boy take with him—and moved them to the barn. The room they had cleared out for the boy's bed gradually returned to its former use as storage for odds and ends. The only visible daily reminders of the boy were the paintings on the barn walls.

"Maybe," Marta said one day, "Jacob is painting a picture of our house and our barn and our animals and pasture."

"Maybe," John agreed, and it cheered him a little to think that the boy might be remembering them.

"And maybe he is making up a little tune right this minute—you know that way he did. Do you think so, John?"

"Maybe."

Another day, Marta said, "Beagle hasn't been the same since Jacob left. Look at him. All he does is lie there. He's sad."

"He's a dog. He's not sad."

"Sure he is, John. Dogs can be sad. Just like people. Just like—"

"Maybe. Maybe so."

Marta lay awake at night, trying to imagine what Jacob was doing. She made up scenes for him. *There he is with his dog. I hope he has a dog. They're running around the yard. I hope they have a yard. There he is sitting on his bed. I hope he has a bed. He's playing his guitar. I hope he still has the guitar.*

John worried while he was driving. *Some people shouldn't have kids. That father shouldn't have dropped Jacob off here without knowing us—what if we were bad people? What if he drops Jacob off somewhere else, where people aren't good to him?* That last thought made John so agitated he had to pull over to the side of the road. He bent his head against the wheel.

45

One Saturday, they returned to the park where Jacob and Lucy had played together, and there was Lucy, swinging, and there was her mother, sitting on the bench, her face tilted toward the sun.

"Oh!" she said, when she saw Marta and John. "What a great surprise! We wondered what had happened to you. We were worried."

Marta explained as best she could.

"Oh, dear. Oh, my. Oh, how very difficult. Oh, how could you bear it? There, there."

The three adults sat for some time, watching Lucy swing. At last, Lucy's mother said, "I know exactly what you should do next!"

46

On the way home, John said, "I don't know the first thing about foster children."

"Me either, but Lucy's mom said those kids need good homes. I can't bear the thought that there are kids out there who don't have homes. Maybe we should talk to that Mrs. Floyd—that friend of Lucy's mother."

"She's in charge of placement?"

"Yes. We'd have to be interviewed and approved."

John scowled. "What if we don't pass? I'm not good at being interviewed."

"Me either. And what if we get a child who isn't happy with us?"

"Or what if we don't like the kid?"

"Of course we'll like the child, John. How could we not like a child?"

"You never met my cousin's kids."

"Won't it be hard if we just have the child for a few months and then he's gone again? Won't that be like losing Jacob?"

"That's the part I'm worried about," John admitted.

"Maybe they won't have any children available anyway. We shouldn't get our hopes up."

When they met with Mrs. Floyd, however, they learned that there were twenty-seven children who needed temporary homes. John and Marta were interviewed and were visited at their home.

"How many can you take?" asked Mrs. Floyd.

"How many? Maybe we should start with just one—"

"How about two? I have a brother and sister who need a home like yours. It's temporary, of course. Be sure you're okay with that. Probably about six months."

47

The brother and the sister who came to John and Marta's were eight and ten years old. Tyler and Zizi were thin as rails and sullen, refusing to speak.

"Jacob wasn't ever gloomy like that, was he?" John asked Marta the first night, after the children were in bed.

"No, never."

"Are we ever going to look after a child who speaks?"

"Shh, they can speak—"

"To each other, maybe, but not to us. They won't even look us in the eye, Marta."

"They're just scared."

"When do you think they'll stop being scared?

Why are they scared? What should we be doing?"

"'Night, John."

By the second week, John and Marta had learned that a pile of old lumber, a hammer, and some nails were a good outlet for the children's aggression.

"What are they making, John?"

"I think it's a fort."

"They sure like to hammer things."

"Jacob didn't hammer. He made music out of everything."

By the third week, Tyler and Zizi were speaking to John and Marta.

"Their language!" John said. "Did you hear what she called her teacher? Where did they learn words like that?"

"Now you want them to *stop* talking?"

"I was just used to Jacob, that's all. I mean he was so . . . so *different* . . . from Tyler and Zizi."

"I guess every kid is different."

It was the goats that finally softened the children. The goats nuzzled Tyler and Zizi and chased them and butted into them. Round and round the pasture the children ran, shrieking with laughter. Early each morning before the school bus stopped at the end of the drive, Tyler and Zizi ran to the barn and fed the goats. Each afternoon, when they returned from school, they raced up to see the goats.

One night at dinner, Tyler said, "It's okay here."

"Yeah," Zizi agreed. "It's okay."

John looked at Marta. "Is that a compliment, do you think?"

At the general store, Shep said, "I see you're buying jelly beans again. That kid come back?"

John felt stabbing heartache. He'd thought maybe he would think about Jacob less with other kids around, but he was thinking about Jacob *more*. He remembered every little gesture, every touch, every look on Jacob's face. When they took Tyler and Zizi to get new shoes and clothes, he remembered taking Jacob to the same stores and how proud the boy had seemed with his new shoes.

"No," he replied to Shep. "These jelly beans are for different kids. We're fostering them."

"Is that right?"

John spotted a roll of tar paper. *That would be perfect for the kids' fort*, he thought. "I'll trade you this here belt for that roll of tar paper," he said.

"You're going to run out of belts pretty soon, ain't ya?"

* * *

John and Marta stood at the fence watching Zizi wrap her arms around a goat's neck.

"You cutie," Zizi sang to the goat. "You cutie dootie."

"You hear that?" John said to Marta. "I think Zizi is turning soft."

"Maybe," Marta said. "Of course this morning, she stomped a caterpillar to bits and called it a *creepy turd*."

"Oh."

"She's a funny kid, that Zizi is."

They could hear Tyler hammering on the fort on the far side of the barn.

"Did you hear what Tyler called you last night, John? He called you Good Pa."

"Is that what he said? I thought he called me Goo-bah. I thought it was an insult."

"Who'd ever guess kids could make you laugh so much?"

"Jacob made us laugh."

"Sure, he did, but I didn't think *all* kids could make you laugh."

"Marta, we haven't seen *all* kids yet."

Tyler and Zizi left one day in the late spring. They'd all

known this day would come, but that didn't make it any easier.

"You can visit us any time you want," Marta reassured them.

"You can write to us, too. We'd like that," John said. "And come visit the goats. They'll miss you."

"So will we," Marta said.

That night, Marta said, "I guess I'm always going to cry when a child leaves."

"Do you think we shouldn't have any more kids here? Do you think we should think about this some more? Are we always going to feel so awful when they leave?"

"'Night, John."

The next morning, Marta called John into the room where Tyler and Zizi had slept.

"Look there," she said, indicating the wall next to Zizi's bed. Zizi had drawn a heart beside this note: *It was okay here.*

"That's a compliment, right, Marta?"

Beneath each bed was a pair of shoes.

"Look at that, John. They left their old shoes behind."

"Makes me want to bust out crying. I found an old pair

of Jacob's the other day, too."

That evening, when Marta came in from planting her vegetable garden, she saw that John had built a shelf on one wall of their bedroom. On it were three pairs of shoes.

48

Children came and children went. John and Marta built an addition on the farmhouse and added beds. The fewest children they ever had at any one time was two; the most was seven. Kids needed homes, and neither John nor Marta could say no when Mrs. Floyd called.

At the general store, Shep Martin said he was going to have to start a whole new store just to stock jelly beans. The manager of the shoe store in a nearby town gave them a permanent discount because they bought so many pairs of shoes.

John added shelves to the original one in their bedroom. There were now twenty-nine pairs of old shoes lined up. Before John and Marta went to sleep each night, they went down the rows of shoes and said the name of each child who had been with them. Many had acquired nicknames; all had left their marks.

"Jacob, Tyler, Zizi, Meggie-moo, Boyd, Sammy-salami, Shayna, Delaney, Bitsy-bo, Luke, Mike-a-like, Hunter, Laina-napalong, Mack, Shareka, Roy-boy, Harry, Jesse-messy, Karlee-darly, Nile, Lily, Oshen, Rosie-girl, Joey, Freddy, Ginny-jumper, Hank, Susanna, and Frank."

Each one had come with a story and each one left a story behind.

"Remember when Mack fell asleep in the truck and we thought he'd run away?"

"Remember when little Bitsy-bo jumped out of the tree and landed on mama goat and mama goat took off and dumped her in the pond?"

"Remember when Lily sang you a song when you were sick?"

"Remember when Freddy and Ginny-jumper tried to make pancakes?"

Some of the children were there a few months, some of them a year or more. Soon after they arrived, they would notice the shelf of shoes and ask about them. Either John or Marta would tell them the story of Jacob, whose shoes were the first on the shelf.

Nearly every child after that wanted to know the story behind each pair of shoes. "And those red ones, whose were those? And the sandals, whose were those?"

And so John and Marta told their stories: they told when each child came and what they were like and how long they were there.

Boyd, a serious nine-year-old, asked John, "And what will you say about me when I'm gone? What will my story be?"

"Well, now," John said, "I'm not sure yet. I won't know until you're gone."

Shareka, a wild-eyed, wild-haired twelve-year-old said, "Tell my story like this: Shareka came to us on a thundery day, and she didn't trust anybody, and she fell in love with a kitten, and she didn't want to leave, but she had to, but she'll come back. The end."

Early one morning, they found Luke and Bitsy-bo on the front porch staring down the drive. Marta thought maybe they were hoping their mother would show up.

"Looking for somebody?" she asked them.

Bitsy-bo, who had green eyes and a perpetual worried brow, said, "Yep."

"You want to say who that might be?"

Her brother, Luke, answered. "We're looking for that boy."

"Boy? Which boy?"

"That boy you found on your porch. The boy that rode a cow."

Bitsy-bo twisted a strand of hair round and round her finger. "He'll be back."

"Oh," Marta said. "You sound so sure."

"Sure I'm sure."

Later that day, Bitsy-bo climbed onto Marta's lap and said, "*I'll* come back."

And she did. Bitsy-bo and Luke visited every summer; Lily, Oshen, and Rosie-girl returned each Thanksgiving. A few were in and out of foster care, reappearing to take up where they had left off.

Sometimes at night, John would say to Marta, "It's okay here, isn't it?" and she would say, "It's a nuthouse, but yes, it's okay here. Yes, it is."

Often they thought of Jacob and often they imagined where he might be. Whenever they were in the barn, they liked to gaze on Jacob's paintings, still there, barely faded.

"Even if we never see him again," Marta said one day, "we know he was here."

"Remember when he used to lie on the porch with the dog? Remember that? Remember his tapping? Remember that music he made?"

"Sure, I do. That boy, that boy. What became of that boy?"

Even on the most difficult days, it brought them comfort to remember the boy who rode a cow.

49

Early one morning, Marta stepped out onto the front porch to breathe in the balmy air, to inhale a few minutes of quiet before all the children awoke. There were now six staying with them and they were an energetic group: Stefania, Jamie, Jock, Ruby, Harley, and Weezer.

The beagle, old now and half deaf, was sniffing the porch floor eagerly, following his nose to a parcel sitting near the door.

"What's that? A package? For us?"

The dog whimpered pitifully.

"Oh, you, dog. You'll get some breakfast in a minute."

It was a flat parcel, about a foot square, wrapped in brown paper and tied with twine. There was no name or address on it. Maybe one of the kids put it there, she thought. Maybe it was something for school.

She forgot about the parcel as she went about waking the children and preparing breakfast, but Stefania found it and brought it inside. No one seemed to know anything about it.

"Open it," John suggested. "Must be for us."

"Oh, I don't know—"

"Open it, open it!" the children chanted. "Open it! Open it!"

And so she did.

John stood behind her, his hands on her shoulders. Both of them stared at the painting.

Finally, John said, "It's the most beautiful thing I ever saw."

"I know."

It was an elegant painting of a boy riding a cow, with a beagle loping alongside.

50

They were not art experts, John and Marta, but the painting looked as polished and professional as any they had ever seen. They would have known its artist was Jacob even if it weren't for the signature at the bottom.

They lay awake most of the night, speculating about how the boy had found them and when he might reappear.

"Maybe tomorrow—"

"—shouldn't get our hopes up—"

"—but maybe—"

"—surely—"

They were alert to every crunch of the gravel drive,

every footstep on the porch.

Could that be him?

As the days and weeks went by, however, with no sign of Jacob, John and Marta alternated between despair and hope.

"Is he gone again, so soon?"

"Will we never see him again?"

"But he remembered us."

"He found us."

"He will come back."

"But . . maybe not."

Marta leaned against the cow, now old and thin. "You hang on, cow," Marta whispered. "When Jacob comes back, he'll want to see you."

The next time John made the rounds in town, he stopped in at the general store, as usual. He had been wondering how Jacob had found his way back to their place in order to leave the painting, and so he asked Shep if anyone had been looking for him.

"Not that I recall, but then, I'm not here every day anymore. I got my son-in-law working up here some days. He's half-worthless, but there you go."

When John walked into the sheriff's office, Darlene, the receptionist, was on the phone. From habit, John scanned the bulletin board.

LOST: that old coon hound of mine. He's run off again. If you see him, call Vernie Gossem, 562-7834.

Absolutely NO dumping in the church dumpster. We mean it!

FOUND: four kittens, cute things, good for mice. Ask Darlene.

When the door opened behind him, John heard the sheriff's voice.

"Well, there, I hear you've got more kids at your place."

"Yep, a real energetic group this time. Good kids, though."

"Don't know how you have the patience." The sheriff slid the back of his hand across his badge. "Still got that old beagle?"

"That's right. Don't suppose anyone's been in here looking for us, mm?"

"You expecting somebody to be looking for you?"

"Naw—sometimes kids need help finding their way back, that's all. Just wondering."

Darlene interrupted her call and held the phone to her chest. "Somebody did."

"That so?" the sheriff said. "Some kid or some bill collector? Ha-ha."

John tried to appear casual. He leaned against the counter. "Somebody was looking for us?"

Darlene held up her finger. "I'll call you back, Flo. Bye, now." Darlene tapped her fingers on the desk. "Howdy. You've got some more kids up there, I hear."

"Yep."

"It's like a revolving door up there, isn't it?"

"Yep."

"Don't know how you have the energy."

"Did you say somebody was looking for us?"

"Oh. Yeah, when was that? Can't hardly remember one day from the next around here."

"Hey," the sheriff said. "Did you ever hear from that boy again? That cow-riding boy?"

"What cow-riding boy?" Darlene said.

"They had a young boy dropped off at their place, years ago, remember that? And that boy used to ride a cow. A cow!"

"I don't remember anything about a cow-riding boy. I can't hardly remember my own name some days."

"Did you say that somebody was looking for us?"

"Oh, yeah, a young college kid—couple of college kids, actually."

"Was one of them a boy?"

"I can't hardly recollect, but I think there were maybe a couple boys and a girl, yeah, there was a girl with them, purty little thing. She did all the talking, asking about you and Marta."

"College kids, eh? And one was a boy?"

"Like I said, yeah, I think so. That was a week ago. Maybe longer. Like I said, I can't hardly remember one day from the next around here."

John returned to Shep's store and bought an extra sack of jelly beans. *Just for old time's sake,* he thought.

And that night John and Marta hung Jacob's painting—of the boy riding a cow—in their bedroom, above the shelves of shoes, where it would be the last thing they saw at night and the first thing they saw in the morning.

51

The old beagle had not been well for several days. He hadn't eaten, and when he was coaxed outside, he merely dragged himself to a nearby bush and lay beneath it, pawing at the dirt as if to make himself a bed. At night, John had to carry him back inside.

One of the children—Weezer—said, "Don't let him die, okay? Let's not let him die."

To Marta, John said, "Don't think this old dog is long for this world. I hope those kids won't blame us if we can't keep him alive."

Marta lifted the dog onto their bed. "It will be a sad, sad day when he's gone."

When they heard the dog wailing the next morning,

a pitiful wail that seemed to come from the hollows of his insides, they feared the worst. The dog was not in their room or in the kitchen. They found him by the front door, weakly scratching at it.

"Let him out, John, the poor thing—"

John had barely opened the door when the dog scooted through the opening, his nails clicking and sliding on the wood. They hadn't seen him move so fast in months.

And then they saw what he was after.

There, asleep in the old cushioned chair on the porch, was a young man, and beside him was a guitar, a paint box, and a blank canvas.

He was back.